MONSTER LIGHT

The Witch Academy of Ash

R.L. WILSON

Cover Designer: Charmaine Ross

Editing: Rainlyt Editing

Proof Reader: Cassie Hess-Dean

Formatting: R.L. Wilson

R.L. Wilson Monster Light, The Witch Academy of Ashes, Book Three June 2021 R. L. Wilson/Exquisite Novelty Publishing LLC

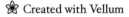 Created with Vellum

Thank you for purchasing Monster Light
Thank you to all my supporters, friends, Arc group, and beta readers for encouraging me, even on the days when I wanted to throw the towel in.
Special thanks to my many mentors. Your mentorship is invaluable. You kept me motivated, gave me advice, and never asked for anything in return. The world needs more people like you.

Special thanks to my husband and kids who stayed up late listening to my ideas and being alpha readers. I hope to make you guys proud of me.

Last but not Least I have to thank God for giving me the strength and the courage to keep striving.

R.L. Wilson

FREE BOOK

Check out my website and claim your free book
www.rlwilsonauthor.com

Or signup for my newsletter:
https://www.subscribepage.com/f2v6g5

BLURB

There's a special cell in Hell with his name on it. It's my job to make sure he gets there.

Under different circumstances, I'd celebrate finding the missing girls and sadistic monster whose held them captive. The monster wants to broker a deal. In exchange for the girls, he wants me.

If I want to send him back to Hell where he belongs, I have to do something, but torture isn't my idea of a good time.

Now I'm shackled and stuck with a fae prince who wants to feed off me for my special magic.

This might be my only chance to get revenge, so I can't blow it.

Time for this disgusting monster to meet his maker.

Find out who wins in this supernatural tug of war in the last book of The Witch Academy of Ash series!

CHAPTER ONE

*P*rince yanks me by my arm, pulling me toward the front of the house. "You think you're slick," he whispers. The thud of the door closing near the back of the house alerts me of Josh's departure.

I don't regret taking their place. The girls wouldn't last much longer. Feelings of impending doom seem to captivate my attention. I stall my footfalls, momentarily thinking I would be tortured or worse if I continue through the door.

He pushes me forward toward the large door. A brass devil graces the front of the door, making my skin crawl. Based on the potent sensation of magic floating around me, I know something is wrong.

Frantically, I dart my gaze around the room,

searching for James. I locate him a few feet away. He's walking away from where I stood, ushered by one of the asshole guards.

Nausea shoots through my abdomen. I look at the door and gag.

"Where are you taking me?" I take a hard swallow.

His fiery gaze beams into my face. "To hell, where else?" he growls.

My lungs stiffen, making it nearly impossible to breathe. Is Prince Lucifer in the flesh?

Fuck that, I'm not going. I kick and swing my arms. He pulls me by my shirt, which is now covering my face. I'm coming out of the shirt.

"I changed my mind. I want to go home," I scream.

"Too late," he says. He pulls my shirt down. My ears catch a click of him unlocking the door. A slither of smoke escapes through the cracks. The door is shut, but there's heat behind it. Hopefully not fire.

I tell myself to stay calm. Punching the air is only making me tired. I must think with my head, not out of anger or fear.

He doesn't touch the door, but it splits in the middle, separating, opening like a giant hole.

I feel as though I'm entering the mouth of a grizzly bear and he is going to eat my ass alive.

"Go on," he says. I stare at the smoke-filled, descending stairs. Hell no, I'm not going.

"Let's go!" he yells. I don't move a muscle. I'm not willing to walk down into that spooky-ass dungeon or, as he calls it, hell.

He grabs me and throws me over his shoulder. I kick, scream, and punch him in the back. Fighting is my first line of defense.

He hauls my ass down the stairs while I curse him, calling him every name except the son of god.

I close my eyes tight, not willing to look. I don't want to see hell. The lower we go, the hotter it becomes. Sweat is racing down my back.

He stops walking downstairs. We're now walking on a flat surface. The heat is almost unbearable as my socks become moist. I peek and open my eyes. Curiosity has gotten the best of me. I see stone walls and a dirt floor riddled with dust. This is worse than what I'd imagined hell to look like.

A dim light exposes the narrow hall. He pauses, then a squeak of a door sounds. I fix my gaze down the hall, noting several other doors. Maybe one leads to the outside.

He enters a room, and the temperature decreases by twenty degrees at least. He flings me off his shoulder and I land on a bed. An enormous bed, I might add. And it's plush, a beautyrest. The hall looks like the dams of hell. But the room has marble floors and a huge bedroom set. It's magnificent, and it matches the upstairs.

"You can't keep me here," I yell.

"You want to bet?" He pulls a chair closer to the bed and takes a seat. He rubs his bruised knuckles, then shoots a glare at me. "Let's get a few things straight. I gave you the best room here because you are special. You got away once, but you won't again."

This asshole doesn't know me. The first chance I get, I'm kicking his ass and getting the hell out of here.

"First rule:" he holds up his index finger, "never call out. If you do, I'll know." He straightens his shirt and I notice several red marks on his arm and his face.

"Second rule: don't try any of your magic tricks or attempt to escape. You'll just be wasting energy."

"Why am I here? What's the reason?" I scream through clenched teeth.

"To fall in love with the prince, my dear."

I turn my nose up and frown in disgust. I will never love him. He murdered Shelly in cold blood. He doesn't have an ounce of love in his frail body.

I twist my gaze toward the wall. I'm done talking. A set of footsteps catches my attention. A give a quick glance, excited he may be leaving. Instead, a lady has entered the room. She wears a maid-like uniform and holds a tray of food. She doesn't stare me directly in the face. But I stare at hers. She appears to be young, likely early twenties, but she looks like a zombie, almost.

Her face is pale, ash-white. She slides the tray of food on a nightstand beside the bed. She glances at me. I view the agony on her face. Her eyes flicker as she parts her lips. It appears she wants to say something, but she suppresses her words then darts a gaze over to Prince. She steps back toward the door, lowering her head.

What has Prince done to her? I can only imagine the torture she must have endured at his hands. *Once I break free, I'll take her with me,* I say to myself.

"Eat. You'll need strength for what I have in mind," Prince suggests.

"Oh yeah? What the hell is that?" I question.

The girl's eyes bulge, and she raises her gaze to

meet mine. Her mouth flies open. She appears to be in shock. Maybe she hasn't seen anyone talk to Prince that way. Or he tortures her. I'm not scared of Prince, but I will be cautious. I'm going to use everything I've learned and beat him at his own game.

A smile curls upon his lips as he rises from the chair. "You must have been born with that smart mouth."

"Maybe," I respond.

He struts toward the door. "Be ready for dinner tomorrow. It will be the two of us."

CHAPTER TWO

I jolt awake with the fear of death gripping my ankles and sweat trickling down my face to my clenched jaw. I don't recall much after Prince left last night. I do remember being scared, so afraid that my harsh breath set my lungs ablaze. I remember tossing and turning all night. Who sleeps comfortably in an unfamiliar place?

I feel like I'm being swallowed whole in the belly of a beast. I must gather a plan and exit this place at once. I sit upright in bed. Beads of sweat break out along my hairline. This is a nightmare I can't wake up from. That queasy feeling pulsates in the pit of my abdomen. No matter how hard I try, I can't stay calm.

This morning, I thought I would muster up

fresh thoughts. Maybe think of a plan. But my thoughts are as blank as a new canvas. I survey the room, narrowing my gaze to the window. The murky light of day fights through the darkness. I suppose it's quite early in the morning. *Breath, Ronnie. Keep breathing. It will be okay.*

I run my hands against the satin sheets, wondering why he gave me such a luxurious room. The hall is decaying. I can imagine what the other rooms are like. What's his motive for keeping me? Turn me into a sex slave or murder me like Shelly? I won't stick around long enough to find out.

Flipping the large comforter aside, I creep out of bed and stalk to the window. I grasp the pane, trying to pry it open using all the strength I have left, which isn't much. It doesn't budge. I give it another hard, swift pull. *It's warded,* I think as I snatch my hand away. Wincing, I narrow my vision on my broken nails.

A sigh exits my mouth. Escaping here will be nearly impossible. I lower my body back on the bed. I stay still, listening for any movement upstairs. There is complete silence. No footsteps or voices. Either no one is here or they are still asleep.

A great time to escape. No one would know.

I dash from the bed to the adjourned bathroom. My bladder is so full my abdomen hurts. A citrus scent masks the moldy, wet scent of the dungeon. The bathroom is quite feminine, decorated in pink with gold accents. The lady servant must have done the decorating. She brought me food last night, but I didn't catch her name. I refused to eat, not that I didn't trust her but because I don't trust Prince. He could poison me. I only drank the water.

After I use the bathroom, I make my way back to the bed. I flick on the television with the volume on very low, barely an audible whisper. This way no one will know I'm awake.

Surfing the channels, I come upon the morning news. I hope someone went to the police and that a search crew is on the way. I watch the news until it ends. There is no breaking news, not about any missing students. Law enforcement isn't looking for me.

Josh knows that James and I are here. He will come back for us. I'm certain of it. But I'm not going to stop trying to escape. The burning desire to be free from my captivity sizzles at the surface.

This castle is enormous. *I have no clue where James is,* I think. A faint knock at the door startles me. It's too light to be a man's hand. I stay quiet, not moving a muscle. Rattling keys sound, then the lock on the door clicks. My adrenaline pumps and my heart beats rapidly. Expecting the worst, I prepare to fight.

The servant enters with more food in her hand and clothes.

"Good morning, Miss," she says. Her brown hair is more than shoulder length. She is beautiful, but the somber looks and sad energy is sucking the life from her.

She sets a tray on the side table and puts clothes and towels on the bed. I note the key ring she has attached to her belt clip. When the time is right, she'll be my escape ticket. We both will be free.

"Prince would like you to wear this dress today. He is requesting you for lunch at 1:00pm," she utters before leaving the room. The smell of maple syrup and pancakes makes my stomach jitter. I have hunger pains that I'm trying to ignore. But there are eggs, bacon, sausage, and hotcakes.

I scoot across the bed to the tray of food. The food looks good; I don't see any visible poison. I grab one pancake and hold it close to my nose. I take a whiff. No bad odor, just the sweet scent of homemade pancakes. It reminds me of my childhood when my grandma made me a hot breakfast on Saturday morning.

I take a bite, chew and swallow it down. I close my eyes; this food is so good. I set the pancake down and wait a few minutes for side effects.

A few minutes pass with no effects. I dig in. I'm hungry as a hostage. After filling my belly, I hop in the shower and put on this dumb-ass dress. It's actually a nice dress with sequins down the sides. Something I would wear to a formal event.

Prince thinks we are just having lunch. I'm surveying this house, making note of all the exits. It's the first step in making an escape. It's imperative I gain his trust. Maybe he will let me be a trusted servant, like the other girl. I don't know what her problem is. I would have fled this castle long ago.

Watching television for a few hours made me sleepy. I'm wracking my brain, trying to remember where the exits are.

Another knock at the door brings me to reality. The knob turns without me saying a word. Prince enters wearing a blue suede jacket and a crown on his head, as if he's royalty. His cocky smile is enough to make me gag.

"Are you ready for lunch?" he questions

"Do I have a choice?" I respond sarcastically.

"No. You look amazing," he says, licking his lips, eyes twinkling with passion.

Suddenly I feel underdressed. I don't like the way he looks at me. Although the dress is elegant and I'm sure it's expensive, I don't want it. I want nothing from him except out of this mansion and him in shackles for murder. And I'll start with my freedom.

"How long do you plan to keep me here?"

"Well, if you cooperate, this will go a lot faster. Maybe you will decide to stay."

This arrogant bastard. I'd never choose to stay here with him. Under no circumstances.

"Let's go upstairs. I've prepared a perfect meal for us." He extends his arm.

I know he is out of his mind if he thinks I'm gripping his hand. After holding his arm out for a couple of minutes, he gets the message.

He lowers his hand and leads the way. I follow him through the post-apocalyptic dungeon as we make our way to the upper level. We get to the second floor and he slides the French doors open to soft music and a lobster meal prepared for two. There are roses and wine.

Has he gone insane? This is not a damn date.

CHAPTER THREE

I survey the room and take the seat closest to the exit in case I have to make a quick dash. Lobster sits on the table filled with fancy china plates and gold linen. I've never been served a fancy meal. I can't say that I'm not impressed. He went through all this trouble to make me a lobster meal. But if he thinks this is some twisted apology for murdering Shelly.... Nope, I'm still kicking his ass when I get the chance.

My plan is for him to spend an eternity in a cell with 24-hour lockdown. His own personal hell, equipped with torturers. That's the least punishment he should get. Shelly's parents won't ever see her again. It must be torture for them.

"Do you like your room?" Prince questions as

he takes a seat across the table. His diamonds are nearly blinding me. No need to get fancy for me. Who is he trying to impress?

"No," I respond. I might as well lie. He doesn't need to know it's the best room I've ever laid eyes on.

"Aren't you going to eat?" he questions while scooping up a fork filled with vegetables.

"No," I respond, stomach rumbling, thinking of the lobster. I have never had lobster before. Where I come from, it's a luxury. We could never afford such a meal.

"Why not?"

"Look, let's cut to the chase," I snap. "Why are you holding me here?".

"I think you're beautiful. But I want to know you better."

"By keeping me here against my will?" I roll my eyes.

"Let me be frank."

"Please do."

He sets his fork down then gives me a sharp glare, one that renders me speechless. If looks could kill, I'd be on the floor right now.

"I'm a dark fae," he says, folding his hands. "You're a light fae."

"That's right," I respond, my mind buzzing with assumptions.

"Sucking the energy from a light fae will give me an extra one hundred human years. I'll do whatever I have to for me and my family."

Shaking uncontrollably, I turn my gaze away from the evil bastard. That's why he killed Shelly. I want him to say it. Admit that he took her life.

"So, you kill light fae witches so you can survive," I grunt through clenched teeth.

"Not kill. Borrow energy," he responds so carelessly.

"You were trying to steal my energy? That night in my dorm room?"

"Yes," he admits. "But I only got a little energy."

"And Shelly?"

"Shelly was a mistake. I was only going to borrow some of her energy, but she resisted. She put up a fight." He lowers his head and his tone. He gives off a sad vibe, as if he really didn't mean it.

"Accidentally, I drained too much of her essence."

"Yes, you took the life out of her," I yell, pounding my hand on the table. I've been battered, bruised, hungry, and homeless. Nothing hurts more than this.

"You need to calm down," he suggests.

"No, I'm not calming down. Shit, you killed my friend for no reason!" I scream at the top of my lungs.

"She resisted and started swinging. It all happened so fast." He pauses. "I'm sorry about Shelly, I really am."

I don't have any empathy for him. Sorry won't bring Shelly back. "You got energy from her and murdered her. What do you need with me?"

"The little energy I borrowed from you was magnificent. It's a premium buzz. Energy like yours is only found once in a lifetime." He stares at me as if I'm a prized possession. A lottery ticket worth a billion dollars.

"I've made everything opulent for you." He narrows his gaze on my face. "You're special."

What is he talking about? "There is nothing special about my magic." I don't even know how to use it. I give him the screw face.

"It's true. Your energy is like liquid gold. My family and I will live for more than a hundred years with just a little of your energy."

Well, they'll die early because I'm not letting

him or his family feed off me. "One question is burning me up. I have to know," I growl.

"Sure, ask me anything."

"Why are pictures of Headmaster Dave in this mansion?"

He flashes his white teeth and gives a giggle. "What, you don't know?"

I shake my head. "What?"

"Headmaster is my father." He pushes his hair back as flames dance in his eyes.

Father. I take in a heady breath as the world around me stops. Everything goes black for a moment before rushing back into focus. That's why I was hauled to jail when he attacked me. "Your birth father?" I question.

"Yes, don't we look alike?"

A mountain lands on my chest. I lean back in the chair. No more news from Prince. I can't handle it.

"I'm only here because you want my energy."

"Yes, but I want you to agree. I don't want what happened with Shelly to happen with you." He stands from his chair and walks closer then sits in the seat next to me. "Besides, I like you." He extends his hand, placing it on top of mine.

"You like the energy I have."

"No." He raises his voice, his beady eyes

burning a hole in my face. "I like you. We can be a couple. You could rule the pack with me, united. A power couple. Imagine a life without worries or bills or death for centuries."

I shake my head no, then snatch my hand from underneath his. "If it means giving up my morals, I don't want that life. Besides, I'm in love with my boyfriend." I raise my eyebrows.

"Oh yes." He slouches in his chair. "Kenny."

"That's right. He's my other half, who is innocent and in jail for a murder you committed." I scowl. "How do you sleep at night?"

"You think Kenny is so innocent? Huh." He rearranges the grin on his face into a frown. "You don't understand half of it."

What the hell is he talking about?

"Your Kenny is no better than me. And if I deserve jail, then so does he."

"No, he doesn't." I grit my teeth and push the lobster dinner across the table.

"Kenny is my runner. How do you assume I know about the new witches? Kenny told me about a new light fae with long pink hair."

I blink back tears. He's lying. It can't be. But his words are like a gut punch. My headache comes back with vengeance.

The stringent scent of death circulates the

room. His words echo through my mind. Kenny is my runner. Kenny is my runner. What does that mean for me? I take a hard swallow of the truth that clogs my throat. Is our relationship real?

I hate the words coming out of Prince's mouth. But it could be true. This isn't news. The twins said the same thing. Did Kenny's guilty conscious cause him to confess?

If what Prince is saying is true, Kenny is in the right place.

Did Kenny set Shelly up?

CHAPTER FOUR

*E*ating a few more bites of the vegetables satisfies the rumble in my stomach. Fuck the lobster. I didn't like it, anyway.

"I'll give you time to think about it."

No need for me to ponder. The flame of rage burns hot in my eyes. We stand, glaring at each other for a few moments. "I don't want to be your feeder." My response is filled with anger.

"Fine," he responds, and his face crinkles into a scowl. "Celena, take Ronnie back to her cell. She needs to come to her senses."

My heart thunders in my chest. I scan every inch of the mansion visible to me, hoping I'll locate an exit to escape.

Celena grabs me by my arm. I don't resist. I don't want to be in Prince's company, anyway. Her grasp isn't forceful. She is just doing as she's told. At least now I know her name. Celena. If she snaps out of the trance, she could be a valuable asset in my escape plan.

I assume he feeds on her. Then again, I'm not so sure. She doesn't have the aura of a light fae. Lately, my senses have been all wrong. I can't seem to separate my internal instincts from reality.

She ushers me down the stairs. I don't put up a fight, no violent kicking or thrashing. It would only make me tired. I need all my energy if I'm going to escape.

The stench of mold permeates the air as the temperature rises twenty degrees. I hear that ever-present voice in my head. *Turn and run.* But I would only get lost in this gigantic mansion.

I try making small talk with Celena. The sadness gracing her face is more visible in the light. I get the sensation that she wants freedom as much as I do.

"How long have you been here?" I question.

She shrugs. "I've lost track of the days," she responds.

It's the first time she's said anything without Prince's presence. She has her own thoughts, but he has brainwashed her. She is almost robotic.

The keys she keeps around her waist are what I'm after. With my help, she will come out of that trance state she's in.

"Is Prince your boyfriend?" I slap my hand over my mouth. I was thinking about it, but it just slipped out my mouth.

She grimaces, turning her nose in the air. The awkward silence hangs around like a foul odor. "I work for him, that's it."

"Holding me against my will isn't work. It's a crime," I grunt before flopping down on the bed. Her somber eyes flicker with tears. "Haven't you ever wanted to escape?" I question.

She shakes her head as tears roll down her eyes. But she didn't answer the question. Somewhere in there is a girl who has lost her identity. Maybe I remind her of the outside world.

She turns away. "I'd better leave now, before he comes looking for me."

I don't want to get her in trouble, but I have to gain her trust some way. This will only work if I convince her to leave, that we won't get caught. I'm going to find James and flee. Prince keeps a set of keys. I'm either getting her keys or his and making a hard run for the door. I take a seat on the bed. I ponder how I got myself into this shit.

I'm just trying to get justice for Shelly. Is that

so bad? A band of sweat forms along my hairline. Feeling faintish, I lie across the bed. My stomach shifts. I close my eyes, trying to stop the spinning sensation. Taking a few heady breaths lowers my heart rate. I'm not sure what's going on, but my stomach is queasy.

A rush of footsteps sound above my head. The pounding of the steps becomes louder as if they're jumping above my head. My hazy vision becomes bleaker. Maybe I just need some cold water.

I rise from the bed. My legs are strong but the pain in my abdomen is sharp. The violent pain stabs at my stomach every few seconds. I rush toward the bathroom. I'm within a few feet and there's another gut-wrenching pain in my abdomen. Rubbing my abdomen, I fall to the floor.

In excruciating pain, I lie there for a moment. Realizing that standing makes me dizzier, I crawl the few feet to the bathroom, heading for the water faucet.

Sweat has drenched my shirt. The cold bathroom floor is soothing. I place my abdomen on the floor, which seems to stop the pulsating cramps. I don't want to get up, but only the weak would stay down. I'm stronger than the pain I'm experiencing. Another cramp overtakes my body, shaking me to my core. I've never felt pain so severe. Each cramp intensifies. My mouth waters and I realize I have to vomit. That slick motherfucker. It was that nasty ass food I've eaten. Did the motherfucker poison me?

I force myself closer to the toilet. Within seconds, a flow of food rushes through my throat, exiting my mouth. That's the last fucking thing I'm eating from this hellhole.

I have to eat to keep my strength. Prince is trying to kill me. I won't go down without a war.

CHAPTER FIVE

J roll over in bed and my eyes snap open. The slight shine of light enters the room. My gaze lands on the small window just above the bed. I think about busting through the window, but it's too small. Not even a child could fit. Besides, it has bars on the outside. I'm caged in and it's worse than prison. At least in prison I had the twins to converse with. Now it's me, day in and day out, staring at the blank four walls. For the first time in my life, I think living in an abandoned building would be better.

Depression has attacked my mind. I don't have time to be depressed. Otherwise, I'll never get out of here. In a few months I might turn into Celena, forgetting what month it is.

Two days have passed. I haven't seen Prince,

only Celena. Small talk with Celena is progressing, but barely. I have gathered that she is supernatural, though I'm still not sure what kind. She attended Mage Academy. She started dating Prince and now depends on him to survive.

He treats her like a servant. She waits on him hand and foot. I can't figure out why she stays here. Brainwashed is my guess. She has keys. Why doesn't she wait until he's asleep and run? But she stays. Maybe she is in love with him. Fuck love, take the keys and vanish. That's not generally the kind of thing you expect from a female, so I can't blame Celena for being scared.

Still, I have PTSD from the violent vomiting. I rub my stomach to calm the growl. I pop the television on, which is all I can do. I'm sick of watching the news. I saw a small headline about me and James once, but since then nothing. People are forgetting about us. No one has even come to investigate.

I surf the channels to find a Lifetime movie. They usually help me escape my reality. But my growling stomach is informing me I need to eat something. I'm only going to eat fruit with a peel on them. Oranges, bananas, and apples. No food that had to be prepared. Prince is poisoning me with food. Maybe an attempt to kill me. That would defeat the purpose if he needs me to feed. I'm paranoid, but I'm not taking any chances.

A tap at the door alerts me. I glance at the clock. Eight am, like clockwork. Celena is here with breakfast and clothes. She slips the key in the lock and opens the door. I can tell by the footsteps it's her. She isn't supposed to talk to me, but we whisper. Initially she was hesitant. Now I'm getting through to her.

She walks toward the bed, tray in hand. She sets it on the side table. Two pieces of fruit are the first thing I notice. Great, at least I have something to satisfy my hunger until lunch.

"Celena, take a seat," I whisper.

"I'm not allowed," she says.

"A few minutes won't hurt." I shoot a sharp stare at her. "Really, I need someone to talk to," I whisper, eager to see her reaction.

She does the unbelievable, and sits in the recliner next to the bed. It's the first time that I've gotten her to have a seat, although I never asked before. I thought she wouldn't consider it. It's one step closer to getting the keys.

"Don't you want out of here? There's an entire world out there."

A somber expression crosses her face. "Sometimes."

"What about going back to school? Living a normal life." If you can call being supernatural normal.

"You don't know Prince." She gives me a firm look, her eyes dancing with fear. "No one leaves Prince," she warns.

I hear her loud and clear. Don't think about escaping or there will be hell to pay.

"I can't stay here forever." I shake my head no. "I'm leaving and when I do I want you to come." I don't care anymore. It's the truth. I trust her. She won't tell Prince, or he will know she is talking to me.

Her eyes bulge. "No," she warns. "It's just as dangerous outside."

"Once we get to the campus we're safe. Then we can call the police," I suggest.

"Are you serious? You're new to the school."

"I am, but..."

She looks to the door and stops talking, listening for footsteps. "Prince has a lot of clout in Chicago. The police won't arrest him. Some of them are dark faes and Prince brings them feeders."

Her whispers bounce off the walls and prick at my eardrums. My mouth twitches as I wonder why no one came to investigate. "How long has he terrorized the campus?" I question.

"Centuries," she replies.

"Centuries?" I whisper in shock. "And the school does nothing to protect light witches and faes?"

She frowns in disgust. "Are you kidding? Didn't you see the pictures of Headmaster Dave upstairs?"

"Yes."

"The Headmaster introduced me to Prince." She repositions herself in the chair. "I went to talk with Headmaster about an issue with a roommate."

"But why? He isn't the headmaster at Mage."

"We have a principal. Headmaster is over all three campuses, though. He suggested I talk with Prince about it. That's how I met him."

Headmaster acted as if he had no clue about who Prince was. That damn snake. I knew there was something foul about him.

"So Headmaster is in on the scheme." I pretend the information is news to me. Prince has already spilled the beans.

My eyes twitch as I take a trip down memory lane. All the crazy things the Headmaster did replay in my head. He claimed he didn't see anyone in my room and had me arrested. He insisted Kenny is responsible for the murder. All this because he is trying to protect his son.

I couldn't contain the anger that is brewing in me. I grab a pillow and cover my mouth while I let out a loud scream. Anger is turning into rage. Even though I already knew it, it doesn't sting any less. I was played like a fiddle.

"I better get going before Prince starts searching for me." She rises from the recliner. The rattle of the keys at her side makes a grin form upon my lips. It's the sound of freedom.

"Calm down. It's not so bad here," she insists.

"Bad? It's hell here," I respond.

The knob on the door turns and fear grabs ahold of my chest and squeezes like a viper grip. I shoot a look over at Celena. All the blood has escaped her face. Fear has turned her face into a ghost.

CHAPTER SIX

eelings of impending doom seem to cut through the air like a machete. The lock clicks and I nearly shit my pants. I fight hard not to scream and remain planted on this bed. The only other person I've seen with keys is the evil Prince so I know it's him. He creeps in, demanding silence with every step. He pauses in front of the bed then darts a gaze at Celena. She is physically shaking. I ease toward the wall, away from the destructive energy.

"Celena!" he yells in an authoritative tone. "Are you on a break?"

She stares at him, not peeping a word. She parts her lips to speak, but she says nothing.

I'm scared for my life, but I speak up. "Yes,

doesn't she deserve a break?" My eyes turn to Celena.

"Quiet," he barks, never taking his eyes off Celena. "What is the conversation about?" he questions. "Me?"

My heart hammers in my chest as I sit helpless in front of this deranged asshole. I'm more afraid for Celena. I'm not sure what he will do to her later.

"We have rules, right, Celena?" he growls

She grabs the bottom of her shirt, twisting it in her hand. Her bottom lip quivers in fear.

"Right?" he screams. His face turns a darker shade of red.

"Right," she responds, covering her ears. She looks like she's standing on train tracks and the train is coming full speed.

The veins in his neck became enlarged. I'm afraid they will explode. Worst of all, I'm responsible for the anger that he may unleash on Celena.

"Please don't blame Celena," I blurt out, taking a heady breath. "I asked her a question." What's the worst he could do to me? Yell? He needs me to feed. I don't need him.

He stalls as the muscles in his arms tighten. He narrows his gaze on my face. I'm in full-on freak-out mode. But a hound like Prince can smell fear. I try to stay as calm as possible.

"So, you run my house?" he says in a monotone voice.

I'm more fearful of the calmness than the yelling.

"No, I asked her a question. She's not a mute. We can talk."

"She can't talk to feeders."

Black lines scatter across his face like cracking ice. I'm not sure what it means. Can't be good for anyone. Damn, what do I do now? "Calm down. I understand we can't talk," I respond sarcastically. "I'll sit in this basement for eternity."

"Celena, leave us at once."

She races toward the door, as if she was standing on hot coal. She didn't blink twice. I've screwed myself now. Prince will never send her down again with food, which means I'll never get my hands on the keys. I can't help that feeling of dread creeping up my legs, shooting through my hands until they tingle. Not like a medical emergency, more like I'll never escape this mansion.

He takes a seat in the recliner where Celena was sitting. The black lines on his face fade, and he returns to his original pale color. The muscles of his body were more relaxed. "Let me make the rules clear again. Apparently, you didn't hear them the first time."

"I heard your rules. But I follow my own. Screw your fucking rules. I didn't ask to come here."

"There are three rules you must follow. If you break any of them again..." He pauses, searing his furious gaze into my eyes. "I'll be forced to discipline you," he growls.

I scowl back. In my head, I'm forming another plan. I'll never stop fighting for my freedom. Besides, he only gave me two rules before.

"Rule one, don't talk with my staff."

This asshole thinks he is some kind of god. He is just plain Prince. There is nothing special about him. He's a filthy murderer. "I know the rules." I bite my tongue so hard it should be bleeding. I want to tell him to go fuck himself. "Is this some type of threat? Because I don't take kindly to threats."

"No, sweetie, it's not a threat; it's a promise." He holds up two fingers. "Two more rules. Can you tell me what they are?" He lowers his hand and raises his eyebrows.

I shake my head no, because I don't care about the rules. I'm going to break them all.

"I'm giving you all these rules for your own safety. You want to live, don't you?"

Frowning, I snatch my attention away from him and turn my gaze to the window.

"Have you considered my proposition?" I sit in silence, ignoring him. He snaps his fingers. "It's impolite not to look at a person when they are speaking to you."

I guess I have no manners, not that I need any. "Nope." I smack my lips, still staring out the window. I know what he's talking about. Will I agree to let him feed on me? Fuck no. I don't care if he or his people die off. Not my concern.

"You don't have forever. If you don't come to your senses in a few days, I will simply take it."

I dart my gaze over to him. His mouth is tight with anger. "Take it? You mean how you took it from Shelly?" I question.

"I told you before. Shelly was a fucking accident. So, stop bringing her name up."

A sharp pain jolts through me. I can't forget Shelly. Every time I see him, her face swirls through my mind. The fact that I'm constantly in the presence of her murderer is revolting.

"I will do whatever I have to for my people to survive," he explains.

"Even if it's murder?" I question.

He lets out a sigh. "Ronnie, can't you see that I care about you? I let no one talk sassy to me. With that smartass mouth of yours, I should have already fed off you without your permission. I want you to see how beautiful it can be if we join forces, unite as one."

That's never going to happen. "I have one question for you."

"Sure, what's that?"

"What did you do with the twin?" I scowl.

"I just asked you to unite with me, and all you can think about is James." He stands from the chair and walks to the door. He pauses, turning toward me. "Remember, you have two days. Make the right decision."

CHAPTER SEVEN

This is not how I imagined life. Always angry, staring into red evil eyes daily. I'm relieved he left. More than ever, I have to leave. Realizing that he will take my energy adds urgency to be freed from captivity. If I knew how to pick locks, I'd be free. He has the doors locked from the inside and out.

Thinking about James makes me sad. I wonder if he's still alive. Or where they are keeping him. Panic like a drum flows through my pulse. I lower myself onto the bed. I grab the pillow and put it over my head. Tears come to my eyes, but I'm not weeping for me. I'm letting James down when he needs me most, and that makes me sick. I have that grim feeling that I will never escape this basement. I'll never see my mother, Kenny, or the twins again.

Removing the pillow, I grab the banana from the tray. Shaking, I can feel my blood sugar drop from hunger. I notice something silver shining from the corner of my eye. I position my gaze onto the recliner. Must be a coin. I bolt from the bed and race to the chair. Snatching the object from the chair makes me sweat bullets. This can't be what I think it is. My hands tremble, dropping the object from my hand. The shriek of the metal hitting the floor frightened me. Screaming on the inside, I rush to pick the object up from the floor. It's a single silver key. I know Celena left the key for me. She wants me to escape. When I come back for James, I'm going to rescue her too.

This changes everything. I wipe the few tears that moisten my cheeks. Gripping the key tight in my hand, I close my eyes. *It's real,* I tell myself. Opening my eyes, I stare at the beautiful key. It shines brightly, like the north star in the inky night skies.

Cautious not to make a peep, I creep toward the door. My moist palms are slick like grease. I nearly drop the key once more, but I manage to stick it into the keyhole. Twisting the key left to the right didn't move the lock. It's extremely hard to turn. My breathing intensifies as I assume this is the wrong key.

Forcing the key left, I push harder, as hard as I can. The key bends as if it will break, then the sweet sound of the lock clicks. I gasp quickly, locking the door again. With excitement in my heart, I grip the key tight. This is my escape ticket. Tonight, after the moon rises, I will make my escape. Nothing is stopping me now. I slip the key into my bra for safekeeping.

My heart lodges in my throat. I forget to breathe. I'm unable to contain my excitement. I'll guard this sacred key with my life. I'm going home. However, this is only the beginning of my battle. Before the sun meets the horizon, I'll return with the police for James and Celena.

The thought of me having a future sends chills zipping down my spine. I can finish school and live my life. A smile tugs at my lips when I think of the priceless look on Prince's face when he realizes I have escaped.

The sky is a dusty gray. Night has fallen upon me. I've eaten plenty of fruit and I'm well hydrated. I have plenty of strength to make a run for it. I stare out at the sky. The night couldn't get any better. But yes, it does. A full moon, shining brightly. The moon will highlight my path through the massive yard and back to campus.

A male guard brought my last tray several hours ago. All I have to do is wait. Once all the movement above my head ceases, I'll make my move. I must be quick and quiet, like a thief in the night.

The noise from the television masks my foot falls. Pacing the floor is tiring me out, but I can't stop moving. Anxiety is overtaking me. If I smoked cigarettes, I would certainly need a pack. Tightening my shoe laces, I prepare for the race. I'm headed straight out the side door. Then I'll be in the race for my life. This plan has to go smoothly; there can be no hiccups or it could get me killed.

Reality twists in time with my heartbeat. I shoot a sharp glare over to the tv. The midnight news came on. I've heard no footsteps above my head for the past hour. It's time to make my move.

Leaving with the clothes on my back and this key to the promise land, I creep to the door, stick the key in, and then snatch it back. My mouth becomes dry as powder. The key seems extremely loud. It's all in my head. I have to do this. A long exhale escapes my mouth as I close my eyes. I slide the key into the hole. Quickly, I turn with a sharp force. I pull the door open then pause. I never knew the door was so damn squeaky. I continue to snatch the door open, hoping no one hears it.

I step into the hall, my heart beating as fast as a cheetah. The thump of my heart is drowning out my thoughts. Wincing, I close the door and take another step. I narrow my gaze to the stairs straight ahead. I only need to make it to the end of the tunnel. One step at a time. I won't be safe until I get off the mansion grounds. Even then, he could hunt me down.

I take another step when a voice splits the air. My heart stops. I think I'm dead. "Who's out there?" the voice says. I twist around. No one is behind me. Another voice sounds. I'm losing my mind.

"Hey, what's your name?" a voice whispers. Okay, I'm hallucinating, but the curiosity won't let me leave. I stalk back toward the voices.

"Hello," I whisper.

Silence at first, then a voice.

"Hi out there, I'm Daphne."

I gasp and walk closer to the doors. Six doors are all lined up next to each other. Another voice speaks, splitting the air. "My name is Mary Jane."

"My name is Rachel. I've been here two weeks, I think."

Horror grabs a hold of me and tears shoot from my eyes. "Hi, Mary Jane. It's nice to hear your voice," I respond, my voice cracking.

"Are you going to help us? My name is Liz. I've been here for a month," she whispers.

He's been stealing girls and hiding them to feed off of.

CHAPTER EIGHT

I crash across the bed, defeated. My entire existence has crumbled to pieces. There's no way I'm leaving these girls behind. I sniffle as a stream of tears drench the pillow. I grab the fuzzy blanket and cover myself. I ball into a fetal position. I want to disappear. But there's no point in feeling sorry for myself. It's not going to rid me of this hell. I close my eyes tightly, tossing and turning for hours, unable to sleep.

An alternative plan is needed fast. What a deranged monster. How many girls has he stolen? What can I do? All the doors are locked. Divide and conquer, that's his strategy. His words replay in my mind. Never call out. He keeps us all separate. Together we'd be strong. I thought he was only keeping Celena. This motherfucker has a gang of girls.

I grab my freedom key and slide it back into my bra. I'm definitely going to use it. I just need a new direction. "You always need a Plan B." Grandma's words ring vividly in my mind. I need plans B and C.

A brush of icy wind graces my face and my eyes bulge. I shoot a stare at the door, but no one is there. I have an eerie sensation that someone is watching me.

My gaze lands on the window. Usually, it's how I tell the time. The morning sun was just rising. I sit up in bed and let out a yawn. I'm supposed to be going to a homecoming game this weekend. However, I'm stuck staring out a single window.

I close my mouth and sit in silence for a few seconds longer. I'll follow my own advice. This will go a lot quicker if I cooperate. That's it, I'll cooperate for the better good. Besides, at this point I have no choice. He said that if I didn't cooperate, he would force me.

I'll pretend to be okay with the feeding. But I'm not. I'll never be okay with it. I'll gain his trust. He keeps a stash of keys on his hip. They must be the keys I need. I'm going to steal the keys and free all the ladies. We will all be free. I'll search this mansion and find James. He has to be here. That dread covers my being. I haven't heard from James. Truthfully, Prince has no use for him. He can't feed off a mage, only the light witches. Why would he keep him?

I have to stay strong. Freedom is within reach. I'm getting the fuck out of here.

The clank of metal sounds outside my room. That's the guard with my tray. So Prince will be here any minute to ask my decision. A faint tap followed by the jingle of keys makes me happy. He never comes in, but I know breakfast is here. He slides the tray on the floor.

When the door closes, I hop up from the bed and scurry to get the fruit. Only one piece of fruit this morning. There is a carton of milk that's closed, so I guess it's safe. As I gulp down the milk, I hear the turn of the lock followed by foot-steps. I set the carton down and stare Prince in his evil eyes.

It takes everything in me not to go off the deep end and tell him I know his secret. Hiding girls to feed on for his personal use. But I bite my tongue for now. My day will come when I can unleash my rage. It won't make a difference to him. But I will feel like a boulder is lifted from me.

His cologne greets me before he does. He has on nice clothes, as if today is special. He takes a seat in the recliner. His perverted gaze rakes me from head to toe, like a lion who's found dinner. I hate him. Even though I'm making my lips curl slightly, it's all a part of my bigger plan.

"Have you made your decision?" He rests his hand on his lap. I notice the shining gold jewelry. Even his cufflinks sparkle.

"Yes," I respond

"What did you decide?"

I try hiding my sigh, but it flies out of my mouth. Force of habit, I suppose. "Yes, you can borrow energy." I give a sheepish smile.

"Great choice," he says as he gazes into my eyes. His smile becomes more pronounced, as if he just hit the lottery. It can't be because I look good. My pajamas are falling off my shoulders. My hair is all over my head. I just woke up.

He rushes from the chair. "I will prepare the ceremony room."

"Ceremony room?" What? We're not getting married. What ceremony is he speaking of?

"Yes, I'm not performing the ritual here.

Someone will come to escort you upstairs. You have time to prepare," he says before marching out the room.

Prepare. He doesn't know me well. I'm going to brush my hair and teeth and call it a day. We're not going on a date. He needs my energy so he can survive. Under no circumstances will his people feed off me. That's a no go.

Slowly, I brush my hair, wondering if I made the right decision. The thought of him feeding on me makes my skin crawl. I feel dirty, as if I was selling my soul to the devil.

There's a knock at the door. It swings open and in walks Celena. My heart leaps into my throat. I want to scream. My mind is at ease knowing he didn't hurt her for me talking to her.

"Hi, Celena." I whisper. She keeps quiet but gives me a hug.

She puts her finger to her thin lips. "I've come to take you to your energy ceremony," she whispers, joy dancing on her face. She is excited to see me too.

"Yes. I'm aware."

I follow her to the hall. Glancing back at the doors, I imagine what the girls look like. Are they being fed or beaten? The hall is as quiet as always. Nothing. I'm sure the girls know not to talk during the day hours. There is a burning desire to ask Celena if she knows about the girls. I'll ask another day.

We pass the main level, heading up another flight of stairs. I wonder how many floors there are in this football field.

We arrive at a large, wooden door with "Prince" in brass letters on the front. I become jittery. I want to race to the nearest exit. My lungs expand, increasing my breathing. I close my eyes. *Stay calm,* I think. She knocks on the door three times, and the door separates, opening like a wide mouth.

CHAPTER NINE

*S*tanding in the doorway, I lift my eyes to the fae Prince, who is sitting on a couch with his leg crossed and an innocent look upon his face. I give him a tight smile before stepping into the room. I'm ambushed by a sweet aroma and soft music, the kind you hear on an elevator in one of those fancy office buildings. He has rose petals everywhere. I'm even stepping on them. The dim light from the candles flicker, highlighting my path to the table that sits in the middle of the room.

What type of ceremony is this? Stalling, I look back at Celena. She nods then closes the door behind me. The patter of my heartbeat becomes louder in my ear. My mouth becomes as dry as a dessert. I hope he doesn't think we are having sex, because I never agreed to that.

He waves me over. "Come on in; I don't bite."

"You sure?" I respond as I continue walking into the room, pretending I'm not scared. I don't want him to know, but my entire body has become hot and sweaty. Frightened is an under-statement. Sheer red curtains adorn the window, giving me the creeps. The room resembles a honeymoon suite. We aren't getting married, one feeding is all I have for this asshole.

"You are special. I want this ceremony to be special for us," he explains in a soft tone.

Nothing about this is special for me. I don't have a choice, or else I'd choose to go back to school. Back to a normal life. Back to when Shelly was alive.

"What's so wrong with us joining forces?" Prince says as he rises from the couch. He's wearing only linen pants, his abs glistening as if he has rubbed baby oil on his chest. He is handsome, I must admit, but I could never see him sexually. He's a filthy monster.

He stalks toward me, almost as if he was float-ing. His essence is calm, more peaceful than ever.

"I find you attractive," he says. He runs his hand gently across my face. He gazes into my eyes in a flirty way, the way Kenny looks at me. Suppressing an eye roll, I step back, removing his hand from my face.

I'm strong-minded, I won't fall for these games. "Let's just get this over with," I huff.

"Wait, don't you want a drink first?

"I could use some alcohol," I respond. Especially since I'm going to be his source of energy. Maybe the alcohol will help relieve some tension. My muscles are tightly locked. I'm deathly nervous. What if something goes wrong? I could end up dead like Shelly. "Yes, a small glass will help. "

"I have champagne. Only the best for you," he says.

He pivots around and heads toward the ice chest. Scanning the room, I search for the keys. They are not on his hip. He never lets them out of his sight. They have to be here. I glance in every corner. There is no sight of keys. Damn. The principle reason I'm here is to steal the keys.

He comes back with two tall glasses of champagne. No way will I drink that much. Last time I got drunk, I couldn't remember shit. And it cost my best friend her life.

I grab the glass.

"Please, have a seat on the ceremony table."

I close my eyes and take a quick swallow of champagne, preparing myself for the unthinkable. I feel like I'm walking into hell with my soul in my hand. What other choice do I have?

Dragging my feet across the floor, I dread reaching the table. This room matches the rest of the house: opulent. I give him the glass of champagne after only one sip. It doesn't taste good and I'm afraid to drink.

He finishes his glasses and gives me a serpent stare. I feel like a caged mouse. Now he is prepared to pounce. "Lay back," he says

I turn and lower my body on the table. My ragged breaths become louder. Each breath is more painful than the last. A tremble sparks from my legs and ricochets throughout my body.

"Are you afraid?" he questions.

"No, I'm not afraid of anything," I respond. I can't let him know I'm horrified. I never thought I feared death. But when you're staring death in the face, fear grabs ahold and doesn't let loose.

He places his hand on mine. I resist the urge to snatch my hand back. The tremble decreases. I'm not sure why.

"I'm a little cold," I respond and move my hand from underneath his.

"I have something for that," he responds.

Shutting my eyes, I reminisce about Mother. I wish I was back home in Wisconsin, living in an abandoned apartment and running from truant officers.

A faint breeze grazes my body and I force my eyes open. He flicks a white sheet then lays it across my body.

"Don't be afraid. It will be painless." He climbs upon the table over me. His face is a few inches from mine. His eyes bore into mine, turning an ocean blue color. The blood escapes his face. He becomes whiter than the sheet.

He parts his lips, but a rumble rocks the table, nearly knocking him to the floor. His eyes widen and he jumps off the table.

I'm not sure what the commotion is about, but I'm glad something interrupted us. Now maybe he won't need to feed.

The rapid footsteps of him rushing toward the door alert me. I bounce up on the table. Before he can open the door, it flies open. A tall, muscular figure stands there. In so much shock my vision is blurry, I blink twice. I can't believe my eyes. Are they deceiving me?

"Prince, what the fuck is this?" that familiar, strong voice barks.

My dream has come true. Kenny is standing before my eyes.

Prince stares Kenny up and down. "How did you get out of jail?"

"Never mind that. What are you doing with Ronnie?" He walks closer toward Prince. Rage crisscrosses his face. "You promised you would never feed off her." Kenny punches Prince and he staggers back.

"Get off the table, Ronnie," Kenny yells.

"Don't you move," Prince growls.

I jump down and race to the corner since they are blocking the only exit.

Prince charges toward Kenny. An all-out brawl ensues. The room is shaking. I can barely see. The dim light is not helping,

Kenny pins Prince up against the wall. "You fight like a bitch," he screams.

There are more rumbles of footsteps. Prince's bodyguards invade the room, grabbing Kenny by the neck. Needless to say, he is escorted out the room and I'm sent to the basement. At least there was no feeding today.

CHAPTER TEN

I bolt awake out of a night terror. A whimpering sound slices the air, similar to the whine of wounded animals. The rumbling commotion assures me I'm awake. I jet from the comforts of the bed then race to the door. The trample of several footsteps rushes past my door. What the fuck is going on? I paste my ear to the door.

"Please let me go," a feminine, high-pitched voice yells. "I promise I won't tell."

"Shut up," a tenor voice yells. It's deeper than Prince's voice. I'm certain it isn't his voice. Maybe a guard.

There's radio silence for a few seconds, followed by a loud scream. I jump away from the door. They've kidnapped another girl. A pain stabs me in the chest. A stampede of footsteps follows, and then a long, piercing scream.

Lowering myself to the floor, I silently cry. There is nothing I can do to help. It's a dagger to my soul. I wouldn't want my worst enemy to be tortured. She continues screaming. Covering my ears, I rock back and forth. I try chanting to myself. I heard none of the girls scream before tonight. It's too much for my heart to bare.

A loud thump of a door slamming sounds. The screams continue, but now more muffled. Soon she will realize the screams won't help. No one will come to save her. They may actually get her killed.

It has been two awful days since Kenny came to rescue me. My patience is wearing thin. I may never get out of here. I stare up at the ceiling and pray to the gods. I want to get back to my life, but my soul won't rest until Prince is in handcuffs, where he belongs.

As long as Kenneth is alive, I know he won't stop fighting for my freedom. That's what love is. In my heart, I know they didn't murder him. He's going to be a big pain in their asses. I just hope he hurries and returns to get me.

I haven't witnessed a peep from the other girls. I dig in my bra and gather the key to my room. Staring at the shiny piece of metal brings peace. I consider sneaking out, having a conversation with the girls. It's a huge risk. I don't want the girls to get in trouble. If anyone ever finds out I have a key, Celena and I are dead. I roll over in the bed and drift back to sleep.

How long can I exist in hell? For a split second, I think death would be better. Maybe Shelly is the lucky one. She doesn't have to fight anymore.

Kenneth knows Prince. But the thought of him betraying me lingers. It's stupid really. He never denied knowing Prince. I'm certain he doesn't work for him.

I close my eyes. Nothing makes sense anymore; I've become delirious. I'm barely sleeping or eating. I'm getting weaker by the day. I'm scared shitless about what Prince may do to me. He hasn't come to my room or summoned me in the past two days. I'd like to keep it that way. I despise being in his presence. The thought of him puts a sour taste in my mouth.

The dreaded knock on the door irritated me. It's breakfast that I barely eat. I guess he wants to keep us alive so he can feed. But he doesn't care if the girls die. He'll just kidnap more girls.

The rattle of the key brings anger to my being. I don't want the stupid food. I just want to lie here. The footsteps stop at my bed. I never acknowledge the person and stay facing the window. "Aren't you going to eat something?" A voice floats from behind me. A crooked grin forms on my face.

I twist around and bolt from the bed. "Celena."

She sets the tray down. "How are you?" she whispers.

"I'm fine," I explain. "What changed his mind?"

"The guards complained, claiming they're not servants. So, he sent me back to do the meals." She grins.

"What happened last night?" I whisper.

"What, the commotion?"

"Yes, a girl. She screamed in agony," I respond.

"I'm not sure. But there is a new girl." She raises an eyebrow. "I can't take her meals yet, though."

I lower my head in sympathy for her.

"Don't worry. This will be over soon." I lift my

eyes to her. "You're strong and defiant, more than the other girls. More than me," she insists.

"How can I be strong? I'm still here."

"You'll find an escape." She winks. "Now you need to eat something; it will give you energy."

Neither of us speak about the key. We both know I have it.

"I'll see you a little later," she whispers before leaving.

I stare at the tray. I don't have a big appetite. However, I'm getting weaker. The bags underneath my eyes have become larger and darker. This place is draining me. I could go insane sitting here every day. I barely have any contact with others. No fresh air or sunlight to touch my body.

I take a spoonful of the oatmeal. It's the first time I've eaten any food in days. It actually isn't bad. It's a sweet cinnamon flavor. After I eat the entire bowl, I take the remote control and flick on the television.

Celena was right. I got a boost of energy. The banana will be a snack later.

I surf through the channels. At least I can watch something instead of sitting here in silence. I assume I'm the only one with a television because I haven't heard any others.

I stop surfing channels when I notice the big red letters going across the screen. The news. I turn up the volume from mute.

"Charlene Anthony has gone missing from Supernatural Academy. Call the campus police if you have seen this girl. She is five feet, five inches with blonde hair and brown eyes. Fifteen years old."

They show a picture of the girl. I cover my mouth. My eyes bulge in sheer horror. She is down the hall in this house of terror.

The police will be on to Price sooner or later. This house is going to crumble.

CHAPTER ELEVEN

*I*t's half past noon, and I sit in bed reading a book. Celena stole it for me. It's my escape from reality. Prince must never find out. It's a self-help book all about conquering the mind. I tap my foot on the floor as I read the book. My eyes become heavy and a sigh escapes my mouth. I lower the book to the bed.

It's clear to me who is in charge here. I need to take my power back. The book says the greats manifested the mind. I have magic. Should've been paying more attention in class. I remember little from class. Nothing that can help me out of the situation. I have to gain mind control over Prince, which is easier said than done. I'm getting out of here, that's for damn sure.

The harsh accusations that Prince made about

Kenny slither into my mind. I'm a prisoner to my thoughts. I'm usually a superb judge of character. Kenny's aura does not scream murderer.

The twist of the doorknob brings the fear of death to me. I throw the book under the bed then pretend I was resting. I never know who is bringing lunch. I will eat a little today, but it won't be much. Usually, I can tell by the footsteps who it is. The guard's footsteps are slower but harder than Celena's, but today they are quick and quiet, different from the others. They stop and before I can turn to face them, the voice of Prince sounds.

"How was breakfast?" he questions.

I twist around and try avoiding eye contact. But I can't. I need to gauge how mad he is about Kenny storming in. He doesn't appear that upset, but his face has fading bruises.

"Your boyfriend stormed into my domain demanding I release you." He scowls.

I sit up in bed and stare his way. *Of course he did.* I stay quiet; I don't want to anger him. Besides, I have a different plan in mind.

"I helped him get released from jail, and this is how he repays me." He walks over to the recliner.

"Why wouldn't he come looking for me?"

He stares into my eyes. "You're right. He's aware of your precious gift."

"Why am I separated from the others?" I question. Damn, I can't keep my mouth together. My tactic to stay quiet fails me again.

A frown graces his face swiftly. "Others? Who have you been talking to? What have you heard?" He perks up in his seat.

"Nothing," I quickly respond and dart my gaze to the wall, avoiding the awkward eye contact.

"You heard something. Who told you? Was it Celena?"

I shake my head no while grabbing the blanket and squeezing tightly.

"That's it. Yeah, it was Celena."

I have to tell him something or Celena will be in trouble. If I say anything about the girls, that's bad for everybody. Shit, think fast.

I narrow my gaze at him. "No, it wasn't Celena. I overheard screams last night. I saw the missing girl on television. It all adds up."

"You did, huh? Maybe you shouldn't be watching television." He massages his forehead with his hand. "Erase the screams from your brain. Got it?" he grunts through clenched teeth.

I nod.

"You should be grateful," he barks.

"For what?" He's holding me hostage.

"That you have a luxurious room. It's only because you're special," he says with a lower tone. His face is less intense. I almost envisioned a glimpse of a soul somewhere in that demon body of his.

He stands. "We're going to finish the feed. This time with no interruptions." He walks closer to me.

I freeze. Is he talking about now? I'm not prepared for this shit. Better get prepared, I guess. He says the feedings will only drain my energy.

I catch a glance of the silver keys dangling from the side of his pants. He'll feed and I get something too.

He takes off his shirt. "Here, you mean." I swallow hard.

"Yes, here and now," he suggests.

I close my eyes and lower my head to the satin pillow. Swinging my legs across the bed makes me think about kicking him in the balls again then taking off, but I would leave the other girls. That's a no go.

I open my eyes to him, spreading a white sheet over me. "Relax," he says as I tremble. "It will only take a few minutes. It will be painless for you."

Trying to ease my mind, I think of school. All I can envision is Shelly's face. I can't help but wonder if this feeding will kill me.

He climbs on top of me, his knees at both sides of my waist, locking me in place. There's no need for him to worry; I won't run. He has something that I need.

He lowers his face closer to mine. "Wait!" I scream, huffing and puffing.

"I haven't even started," he claims.

I'm sweating. "I know." I lift my head from the pillow. My chest rises and falls rapidly.

"Stay calm. This could have been over by now."

I lower my head back to the pillow and get mentally prepared. "Ok," I respond, my inhale sharp and painful as if something is piercing my lungs with a knife.

He lowers his face to mine and opens his mouth. I part my lips in response, unsure if that's what I'm supposed to do. Within seconds, a warm sensation tingles in my stomach. It's like warm blood slithering up my chest and out through my esophagus. It doesn't hurt, but it makes me warm and shaky.

The warm sensation flows out my mouth for several minutes. I become weary, more and more drained. Just before my eyes close shut from the fatigue, the sensation stops.

Slowly, he rises off me. I catch a look in his eyes. They're glowing a red color, blinking on and off. His face has large gashes that open then close repeatedly. He rolls over in the bed with a grin on his face. He appears stoned.

What the fuck just happened?

CHAPTER TWELVE

The creepy sound of the door opening brings a pounding to my chest. I flip my gaze to the right, feeling the warm body beside me. I'm certain it's Prince, but who is entering?

There is a steady stream of footsteps, as if they are coming from afar. However, the presence is inside the room. My eyes are glued to the entrance, awaiting someone to appear. Nothing. The footsteps cease.

It was my imagination, I think. Now is my time to escape. A quick peek at Prince reveals deep frown lines and a deep sleep. The keys are mine. I flip the sheets back, preparing for my escape. The footsteps sound again. Glancing at the door, I'm shocked at the tall figure looming.

"James," I yell. "How did you get in here? Where were you?" My mouth moves so fast, I don't have a second to think. He holds a finger to his lips, quieting me. I almost forget that Prince is here.

The sexy smirk on his face is enough for my panties to ignite in flames. Now isn't the time for passionate sex. I just want out. He continues floating toward me, not saying anything.

"We have to go," I whisper as I scoot to the edge of the bed, careful not to wake Prince.

"Yes, beautiful." He takes a seat next to me. My gaze catches onto his brown eyes. He gently runs a finger across my cheek. I'm burning with passion.

I hold back a grin, attempting to be serious. My eyes trail his chiseled chest down to his belly button. He entered wearing nothing but a pair of dark denim jeans. A bold move inside of Prince's mansion.

I flip a glance over my shoulder to assure Prince is still sleeping. Nobody is there. Quickly, I glance back at James. His face shines bright like the North Star. "Where did Prince go?" I question, nervous about his disappearing act. Will he reappear, catching me and James together? That could be our demise.

Again, James shushes me, grabbing my attention, keeping it on him. He kisses my lips, and I don't revolt. My instincts say this is wrong; I've already been with Josh. But my desire for James has grown. It's strong as a wild beast. No longer can I tame the need for his touch.

I feel safe in his presence, secure. I forget about yesterday or tomorrow. Time stands still. All I need is right here. I want to lick him like a fudge sundae on a summer's day.

My mind says run now. Together we can make our escape. But my hands are already assisting James in taking off the few pieces of clothing he's wearing.

I give him that look of panic. He kisses my forehead and then my lips. Fuck it, I want him. My panties are soaked from the tingling sensation, my essence flowing like a river from his gentle kisses.

He unbuttons my pajama top and plants kisses across my clavicle then downward to my breast, stopping at my nipples. He sucks gently at first, then harder as my panties become moist.

I lay back in bed as he crawls in behind me, naked and erect. His penis is as big as a python. No way will it fit, but I'm determined to expand to fit him.

My legs slide apart, welcoming his manhood. I need him inside of me to put out the inferno. He runs the head of his penis up and down my vagina, teasing me. Gently, he thrust his penis in. I've never had a more pleasurable pain. I moan for more as he pushes again and again. There is an explosion of my essence. I want more. I have been anxiously awaiting sex with him for months. He doesn't disappoint.

I flip him over, about to give him the best ride of his life.

I gasp and snap awake, breathing heavy. The sheets are soaked. Did I urinate in the bed?

CHAPTER THIRTEEN

My eyes jolt open. Sweat is beading down my face, and I'm shivering from my wet clothes. I stare up at the ceiling. Damn, that was quite the wet dream. The sheets are drenched in my essence. It's cool and sticky, racing down my inner thigh. I exhale and smile at the thought of sex with James. I roll over to my side, forgetting where I am.

Gasping, I stare into the face of Prince. That wasn't a dream. Well, the sex was. The feeding was real. I ease the covers off my body, my heart hammering in my chest. Now is my chance. Slowly, I ease out of the bed. I'm going to steal the keys. My legs wobble beneath me as I attempt standing.

My feet are like two-ton weights, and my eyes are even heavier. I'm drained, like I just had a major surgery or mind-altering drugs.

I take one step, shuffling forward. I move with urgency. Jackpot. I locate his trousers on the floor next to the bed. I'll grab the keys and get the hell out of here. A spike of pain rattles through me, but I ignore it. I can make it. Only about eight more steps.

The bed squeaks, sending an icy chill down my back. I pause, not moving a muscle. I dart my gaze to the bed as Prince turns over and grinds his teeth. He's in a deep sleep. It's now or never.

I force my feet forward. Pain surges through me, which only forces a low groan. I lower myself to my knees. Frantically, I rifle through his pants pockets. Searching the front pockets, I find nothing. *Shit,* I scream internally. A feeling of impending doom sets in my chest, wrapping around my heart like a python. My internal instincts urge me to shake his pants. I give the pants a slight shake and metal rattles. Immediately, I stop, not wanting to alarm Prince.

My breathing increases. My audible breathing is going to get me caught. I can't compose myself. Reaching in his back pocket, I locate a handful of keys. I want to scream. A joyful noise. *Calm down.* My hands tremble. Suddenly, the urge to urinate is pressing. But there's no time; I must escape.

Adrenaline pumping, I stand to my feet. I'm still unsteady, but the thought of freedom makes me move quicker. Standing at the door, I shut my eyes. The door always makes a slight noise when it's opened, and I'm afraid the squeak will awaken the asshole. Exhaling, I wipe the sweat from my palms, then grip the door knob and give it a swift turn, not looking back.

I exit the door and head toward the next room, determined to free everyone, including Celena. She's been his servant at his beck and call. I'm still confused about why, but I know she wants freedom too.

I arrive at one of the doors and fumble through the keys. They are blank, no room numbers. Which one should I choose? It's a ring full of silver keys. I have to be patient. I start with the first key. My hands are still shaking trying to get in the hole. It doesn't turn. Next key. That one doesn't turn either. Dammit! Come on.

Scanning the key ring, I notice three keys with skull heads engraved on them. These have to be the keys. But which one goes to this door? I slip the first key in and the lock clicks. My eyes jolt. I'm afraid of what's behind the door.

I push it open. Two bright eyes stare back at me from the darkness.

"Who's there?" a faint voice says.

"I'm Ronnie. I came to rescue you," I whisper while searching the wall for a light switch.

I flip the light switch, and the light exposes a frail girl. The scent of mold permeates the air. I notice her long, greasy hair. It nearly touches her elbows. She sits in the bed with her head buried into her knees. The room is nothing like mine. Brick walls and a bed. No window or television. A torture chamber.

"Go away," she barks.

"Don't you wanna go home?"

Her gaze peers toward me and she pushes her hair back. "We'll never make it out of here alive," she growls.

"Don't you want to try?" I whisper.

She flips a glance behind her as if someone is watching. "I'm terrified. I gave up going home months ago."

"Now is our chance." I hobble toward her, careful not to make any sudden movements. I don't want to frighten her. I extend my hand.

She nods yes, placing her hand in mine. "I'm already dead sitting in this cell."

She rises to her feet. We head to the door, leaving the filthy room behind. Now to free the other girls.

Arriving at the next room makes despair gnaw at my guts. I want to free all the girls, but my internal clock says we are running out of time.

This room is like the last. When I get closer to her, she nearly jumps into my arms. She wants to escape. "Hello," she says. I recognize her voice. Mary Jane.

Now the last door. We're so close to freedom, I can smell it. My bones chill with the thought of freeing all the girls. I open the last door. The face of Jenny stares back. It's the girl whose face has been plastered over the tv for days.

She hops to her feet in a defensive stand, ready to brawl. Dirt covers her right cheek. "No, I've come to rescue you."

"Is this a trick?" Her voice whips me back.

I pinch the bridge of my nose, trying to drown out the awful smell of urine. "The other two girls are waiting outside these doors. We will all leave together."

Initially, she's hesitant. She creeps to the door,

staring me in the face. She eases her head out the door. Swiftly, she glances back at me. "Let's go!" she squeals loudly.

"Shhh," I whisper, putting my finger over my lips.

I follow the others up the stairs. The warmth of the heat grazes against my cheek. The pulsating power of magic becomes stronger. I sense that a supernatural is nearby. I don't have the nerve to tell the girls. We will keep going until we can't.

Everyone moves quicker than me. My mind is racing, but my body is slow to respond. A side effect from the feeding, I assume.

We can't alarm Prince. As we near the top of the stairs, the line stops. Jenny waves me up front. Maybe she is afraid to keep going, but I'm not. I'll find Celena and she'll lead us to the right exit.

I'm almost certain her room is on the first floor. If not, we are screwed.

We move through the house like thieves in the night. I stop at the hall and tell the girl to wait. The terror on their faces makes me cringe. It will be worth it once we are free.

A flash of James comes to mind. I'll send the police for him. Prince can't feed off him. He'll be okay, I reassure myself.

I'm slow to turn the knob. The horror of me entering the wrong room consumes my thoughts. I have to take a chance. I've flirted with danger my entire life; there's no point in stopping now. Here goes nothing.

CHAPTER FOURTEEN

*T*he stillness frightens me the most. The room is as quiet as death. Either I picked an empty room or it's someone else's. Terrified of flicking on the switch, I stand quietly and listen for any signs of life. The whispers of the girls are audible in the background.

After a few seconds, the bed squeaks. My spine jerks upright. I pivot around as fast as my feet will move.

"Hello." A voice sounds. I let out a heady breath of relief. The voice is raspy but feminine, the sounds of awakening from a deep sleep. But it's Celena. I feel comfortable to hit the light switch, but I didn't.

"It's me, Ronnie," I respond. Heavy breathing and quick movements follow.

The light flicks on and Celena stands before me in a frenzy. Her bottom lip quivers as a deep frown creases her brow. She places her hand over her chest as if she is clutching invisible pearls. "W-w-what?" She is so flustered she could barely get the words out. A worried expression mars her face.

"We're escaping now. I came for you." She puts her hand over her mouth. Her hands tremble like she has Parkinson's. Without a second thought, she races toward the closet and grabs a pair of sneakers.

Quietly, we sneak toward the main room. I'm more confident with Celena leading the way. I was leading out of fear, but Celena knows this house and every exit.

Celena lays her eyes upon the other girls. Her furrowed brow tells me she is beginning to worry.

"It's okay. We have to go now," I urge. Celena's breathing only becomes more labored, like an asthmatic patient. I grip her by the arm then give her a shake, trying to knock her back to reality. Or at least knock the fear of death out of her. The face she makes sears a permanent spot in my head. I pray I'll never witness that look again. She has the appearance of a girl who just stepped out of a grave.

Slowly, her color returns to her face. She points north. "This way," she says, walking quickly toward the back of the house. Her small feet driving into the floor is making a rumbustious noise. She's eager to escape, just like the rest of us.

After several more minutes of trotting through the house, we go down another level of stairs. The mansion is one big maze. I thought we would never make it. In reality, it's a few minutes. But when you're running for your life, those minutes feel like days.

We stand staring at the door. It's only a few feet away. The face of James crosses my vision again, almost as if he is standing before me. But I know it's a hallucination. It's impossible for him to be here. I shake my head, pushing away the vision. It's difficult to leave him.

"Ok, ladies, we're almost there," I whisper. "Celena." Her face is brighter than a kid on Christmas morning. The other ladies stand behind her. Celena reaches into her bra and grabs a set of keys.

She inserts the key. The lock opens, making a slight noise. But it sounds like a chapel bell in this mansion, echoing off the walls. She swings the door open. The wind takes my breath away. It's the first time a breeze has crossed my skin in days.

One by one, the girls follow Celena to freedom. I get right outside the door, when I'm suddenly yanked backwards and thrown to the ground. My vision is hazy, but my fist is swinging. "Run! Run!" I scream, hoping the girls will get away.

I focus my vision, realizing I'm not hitting anyone. I lie on the ground. In the distance, I see the girls running toward the back gate. The yard is like a park. They are halfway to the gate. Prince watches the girls as his face becomes as red as the devil. He pulls a golden lamp from his pocket. It's a genie lamp. Not sure who it's for.

He's not catching the girls now. My heart triples in speed at the thought of the girls being free. I try standing on my feet with my eyes glued to Prince. I turn to make my escape in the opposite direction, but run into the chest of a tall, muscular asshole guard.

An eerie sound snatches my attention. It's a screeching noise, as if someone ran their nails down a chalkboard. It sends a chilling sensation to my bones. I narrow my gaze on Prince as he continues rubbing the lamp, which is making that awful sound.

Right before my very eyes, I witness Celena being warped into the lamp until her essence is gone. She's vanished, hidden in the lamp. I gawk as my stomach drops. I never knew she was a Jinn. Did she gift Prince with a fortune?

The girls never stop running. Blake the guard grips me by my hands and throws me back into the house. I might be a captive for now, but at least the girls are free.

CHAPTER FIFTEEN

a fist comes flying at me, whacking me in the face. I stumble back and cross my hands over my chest. He reaches for my arm and I cock him in the face. I got a hefty blow in. There's more where that came from.

He snatches my arm, pinning it behind my back. I flail and hit him in the mouth this time. He snickers. "Is that all you got?" He snatches me by my hair and drags me into a cell. It's like a prison cell but worse. There's not even a cot to lie on. And no toilet at all. It's dingy and filthy. Just looking at the inch-high dust makes me cough.

I plead to be set free, but no one hears me. "Let me go!" I scream to the oversized guard. He throws me to the cement floor then heads for the door. "You can't leave me here. I'll die," I insist. It smells like a skunk died here.

Out of the dark shadows appears Prince. His angry snarl makes me panic. But I can't show any fear. Fear will get you killed. He stalks toward me and my body tenses. I tried being strong. But with the angry expression on his face, he's likely to kill me.

He bends his knees, lowering himself to the ground.

My eyes jump and blink out of nervousness. I'm a savage, but I'm still a girl. I'm not scared of him hitting me. I'm more afraid of the torture brewing.

"You ungrateful bitch!" he screams in my face with force. The veins protrude with wrinkles on his forehead. He's furious.

"I gave you everything," he spits.

I close my eyes. My heart is dancing with fear. I've never seen anyone so angry. The steam rolling from his head looks like he might explode any second. He grips my arm, squeezing tighter. I open my eyes. His eyes bore into mine. Rage is oozing from him. I don't care what the punishment is. I'm not sorry I freed the other girls.

"I could kill you right now with my bare

hands." His grip becomes tighter around my arm. I grimace, inching my arm away. He yanks me closer. I keep quiet, not wanting to anger him more. "You fucked up. I will feed on you and only you," he yells into my ear.

Panicking, my magic buzzes, thrumming through my blood. It's the worst time for it to show up. I needed my magic ten minutes ago, when I was getting my ass dragged down the stairs. Within seconds, my arms burn, sending an electric spark through my body.

He drops my arm, snatching his arm back. Whining, he rubs his hand on his trousers. "Oh, you're going to use your magic, witch?"

The bodyguard stalks closer into the cell. I shoot him a murderous glare. Prince holds his hand up, telling his body guard to stop. I notice the red mark on his hand.

"You will sit here and rot," Prince grunts. "That's the price for freeing the others. Celena will be trapped inside this lamp for a thousand more years."

I turn my face away as I feel tears burn the sockets of my eyeballs. Celena may be in a worse place. I failed her. I'll commit suicide before I let him see my tears, though.

He walks away, then the rattle of the door echoes. It's a large, steel door with a tiny window and a slot they can slide trays through. No way my magic can burn through a steel door.

This is for animals, I think as I lie on the concrete floor. The dim light flickers on and off. I bury my face in my hands. The flood of tears explodes. I tried holding back, but it's inevitable. There's no way out. I burn hot. Maybe I'm having a heart attack.

The girls won't leave me. They will return with a magical army. But I also thought Kenny would be back, and he never came.

I wonder where they are holding James in this place. After soaking in my misery for several minutes, I stand to my feet like a powerful witch does. I dart my gaze around, looking for any way out. An object to break the glass on the door. There's nothing.

I walk to the door then jump up to the window. Nothing but more bricks. I bang on the door. Fuck. I reach into my bra, retrieving nothing but lint. I lost the keys in the shuffle.

I notice a blanket laid on the floor in the corner and I race over to investigate. The blanket is a gray fuzzy one. It looks like a child's blanket. I hadn't noticed it when I first came in. I bend over and pick it up, then take a sniff. It doesn't have a funky odor, but it doesn't smell like Downy either.

There's nothing under the blanket but concrete. The spot is cleaner than the rest of the floor. I assume this blanket has been sitting here for some time.

Since it's freezing in here, I will use the blanket to warm up. Sitting on the floor, I rest my heavy eyes. I have grown weary of crying. I just want it all to stop. The guilt of sending Celena back to a lamp. Leaving James behind. The fact that I may be here for the rest of my life. If I had a razor, I would end it all here on this floor. I close my eyes and nod off, quieting the thoughts in my head.

A rattling at the door awakens me. I sit up, trying to appear as if I wasn't sleeping. The noises cease momentarily. Maybe I was dreaming.

A bang at the door causes goosebumps to race down my arms. That asshole is back. I suck in a breath, preparing for him to enter. Then there's another loud bang on the door. Wait, that can't be Prince. He has keys. Whoever is at the door is mad as hell.

The pounding becomes louder, one after another. I scurry across the room, searching for a place to hide. Whoever at the door is breaking in. I hope I'm not the target of their anger.

CHAPTER SIXTEEN

*S*everal drops of sweat trail down my face, working their way from my blonde hair to my neckline. I cover my ears, closing my eyes. But they keep plowing toward the door. The hinges rattle. I rock back and forth. Are they going to kill me? What will I do? There's nowhere to run or hide.

With a savage growl and another swift kick, the door flies open. I keep my eyes shut tightly, not willing to view the monster. What got him so enraged? I'm trying to summon my magic. If all else fails, I'm going straight hood. I'll use my fists.

"Ronnie, it's okay," a male voice says. A familiar voice of love. Kenny's voice. I open my eyes wide. He is standing there in the flesh. I'm not hallucinating. He came back for me.

A sudden whimper escapes my throat as I struggle to breathe. The grip of Kenny's hand on my arm stops my panicked breath. Kenny's touch brings a peaceful presence. I know I am safe. Everything and every sound disappears, even my loud, racing thoughts. I extend my hand, touching his chest, and then move my hand to his face.

He grabs my hand. "I'm real."

"What, how?"

"Don't worry." He plants his soft lips on mine.

I breathe a sigh of relief, tears filling my eyes. I know the biggest battle is ahead. We have to escape this mansion alive.

"We're leaving. Even if it's over Prince's dead body." He nods.

I'm uncertain why Prince hasn't appeared. Has Kenny already killed him?

"I'm glad you're okay." I catch a tenor voice somewhere nearby. Josh steps out from the darkness, his eyes bright with excitement. My stomach knots as he walks toward me. The light blinks, exposing his handsome features. I glance over at Kenny to see his reaction before I respond.

The presence of love still graces his face. I know it's safe to show my feelings. "Hi, Josh," I respond, overly excited. Josh kneels and kisses me on the forehead. I try standing on my own. Kenny grabs hold of my arm, assisting me.

"James is here too. We'll find him," Josh insists.

"Wait." I look Josh square in the face, suppressing my fear. "I haven't seen or heard James the entire time I've been here." I grab his hand. "Be prepared in case he is dead."

He frowns, turning his nose in the air. "No, he can't be."

I know the word dead is hard to hear. It's hard to say, but it's quite possible. "Maybe."

"Impossible. My twin sense has located him. It's faint but here."

"Alright, let's go," Kenny urges

We trot out of the filthy dungeon and I still feel imprisoned like a slave. I won't be totally free until we make it out of this castle of doom.

Kenny seems relaxed, almost too calm. It doesn't bother him if Prince comes. He isn't whispering or creeping about the house. "We have to be quieter," I insist.

"No need," Kenny states. "I have an ass whipping with Prince's name on it."

I push the dreaded questions to the back of my mind. Prince said that Kenny brought Shelly to him. Everyone can be forgiven. I really need the truth.

We continue down the tunnel, heading for the stairs. It's the only exit, which means we have to defeat Prince and his entourage.

"Here. Right here," Josh says. "James is behind this door."

We freeze in place. I see the old wooden door. I'm in disbelief. It's feet away from where I was held. I never noticed it before. But every time I passed through here, I was in fear for my life. That way it seemed invisible. If Josh wouldn't have pointed it out, I would have walked right past. The black handle blends in with the wall.

Kenny grabs the handle and pushes. The door is locked or warded.

"James," Josh yells.

No answer. Radio silence. *Is he sure this is it?* I think. He has a twin sense. I'm not going to argue with his instinct.

"James," Josh yells again.

Kenny kicks the door repeatedly. He doesn't even put a dent in it. I realize the door is warded. Even if I had the keys still, they wouldn't work. There's only one solution: force Prince to break the ward. But that's easier said than done.

I place my hand over my head. We're helpless. There's no way Josh will leave without James.

"I'll search for Prince. He'll open this door," Kenny explains as he heads down the tunnel. Josh and I watch as he disappears into the darkness. "Don't worry, Josh. "

"I'm not," he says.

But by the shakiness of his voice, he's worried. The thrumming of my magic sizzles at my finger-tips. It's slightly annoying. I cross my hands over my body, trying to stop the buzzing. Nothing happens. I flick my hands out and a jolt of energy releases from my hand, like an invisible wave of magic. Josh jumps back and my hair sways left. The magic busts the lock and forces the door open.

I glance over at Josh with fear on my face.

"Yes. I felt that," he says as he inches toward the door.

I gasp and step back. I let Josh enter first. Besides, he's the man.

"James," he calls as he shudders forward. I follow behind in Josh's shadow.

A lamp sits on the bedside table. James lies in the bed. He appears lifeless, but I can't let Josh know how I feel. We stalk closer and he still never makes a sound. *Is he dead?* He's not moving.

We stop in front of the bed. Both of us are afraid to touch him. His pale face has a grin, a cheerful grin, as if he's somewhere else. I can't dare look at Josh. I can't see the grim expression of pain. My lungs stiffen.

I grab Josh's hand with my eyes glued to James. "We have to go," I whisper.

He moves in closer and nudges James on his shoulder. "Come on, James, let's go," he squeals.

I'm not sure what to do. It's awkward as hell. Should I leave and give him privacy? Or stand here in silence? This tragedy is pushing me to my breaking point. I have lost one friend at the hands of Prince. Now another one. His soul is required in hell.

Josh drops my hand. "Come on," he says. Tears jerk from my eyes. I can no longer hold it in. I turn to leave.

I flip one last glance over my shoulder at James. My way of saying goodbye. A slight movement of James's hands shakes me. My eyes must be deceiving me. But then his hand moves again as his eyes flutter. He parts his lips, hyperventilating, taking in deep breaths. He glances at Josh. "How did you find me?" He takes in several more heady breaths.

He smiles and tries sitting up in bed. I notice

fading bruise marks up his arm. I could imagine the torture he has suffered. At least he's alive and we all are leaving this house of horror.

"Are you okay?" I question.

He grins. "Now that I see the two of you, I'm fine." He gets out of bed, assisted by Josh. A thunderous crash rings out above our heads.

CHAPTER SEVENTEEN

*T*he rumble above our heads is a sign. The reaper of death is here for our demise. Evilness burns within the soul of Prince. He will attack us. The twins appear just as horrified as I am. My pounding heart confirms that I should be afraid. Yet, I tuck that fear deep down inside. So far down inside, no one will locate it. I've proclaimed freedom for myself. No dark fae is going to strip me of that.

Another crash causes the mansion to shake. The twins take off, racing toward the commotion. Josh in the front and James behind. James has a slow takeoff, yet he is moving faster than me, even though in my head I assumed I was as fast as a cheetah.

If we're going to live, we have to bind together

to take on Prince and his entourage. I have only seen one asshole of a guard, but he is huge. Much bigger than Prince or Kenny.

The guard should go to prison too. He is as guilty as Prince. I'm sure he feeds off the girls too, but he hasn't fed off me.

I muster enough strength to get up the stairs. Josh made it minutes ago. Before I get through the door, another loud boom like an explosion sounds. I want to run toward the explosion. I force my feet to move as fast as I can. Glancing toward the men, there is a full war happening. I can't make out who everyone is, but surely, I see Kenny. His bright orange shirt gives him away. His face is pinned to the floor. There are at least five guys fighting.

I don't know who is who, but Prince doesn't appear to be in the mix. I groan as a grim sensation pulsates in my chest. The large fist of the asshole guard drives into the face of Kenny. I need to do something, before he kills Kenny.

A gust of wind flies beside me as I witness James join the brawl. Seeing his twin on the opposite end of double-fist power-drilling into his body gives him the strength that was lost. He dives into the fight. There is Prince. James snatches Prince by his ponytail then drives his head into the wall, breaking through the plaster.

I want to help, but what should I do? My magic seems out of commission. These men are bulky and strong. I won't leave my guys, no matter what happens. But so far, we are getting our asses kicked. I grab a handful of my blonde, stringy hair, wrapping it around my fingers as my bottom lip quiver.

I have the urge to vomit. My stomach shifts. I don't know how long I can stand here and watch. Fuck it, we can all go down together. I charge toward the bulky asshole who is pounding on Kenny. Jumping on his back, I dig my fingernails into his eyes, scratching into them with all my might. He stands, flailing around. He let go of Kenny, which was my intention. But now I'm holding on like I'm riding a bull. I keep my grip on his eyes. He lets out a loud squeal and moves around in a snake-like motion, throwing me off his back. I slam into the wall. The world becomes wobbly.

Once I regain a stable view, I see the guard covering his eyes and Kenny getting off the floor. His shirt is torn to shreds. His chiseled chest is covered in angry red bruises. He huffs and knees the guard in the stomach. Eyes still covered, the guard bends over, moaning in pain. That doesn't stop Kenny from punching him in the back with several blows until the asshole falls to the floor.

Meanwhile, Josh is getting his head rammed into the oven by one of the guards, one that I have never seen before. Enraged, I close my eyes as my magic thrums through my veins.

Kenny races to my side. "Are you okay?" he questions.

I nod, unable to talk out of anger. I open my eyes to see the huge guard charging toward Kenny, power-driving him into the window. It happens so fast, within a blink of an eye. Not even a second to react. The glass shatters into a million pieces, before Kenny and the guard fly to the ground.

My magic is so strong it nearly suffocates me. My body feels as if it's stretching. There's no pain; just an overflow of anger directed at Prince and his minions. I locate a knife on the counter. I stare the knife down. I'm determined to grab it. I rise to my feet and head across the kitchen. Before I reach the sink, the knife flies across the room, stabbing the bodyguard beating Josh in the back. I cringe as my heart nearly falls out of my sock. A scream exits my mouth. Fuck, did I do that? I was thinking about it.

The guard's shirt becomes saturated with blood. I still don't feel any sorrow. He releases his death grip from Josh, who's barely clinging to life. Josh's shallow breaths and fading color only angers me more. The smoke streaming from my hands slowly burns. It needs an exit. I flick my hands to rid the pain from my hands. Bolts of sizzling magic jump from my hands, attaching themselves to the curtains, setting them ablaze.

I'm relieved all the bottled anger is released. Prince is now on the floor with James straddling him.

"Stop. Stop. Let's go." I rush to Josh, helping him to his feet. James hops off Prince and rushes to Josh's side. We wobble to the door. I pause. There's something I'm forgetting. I pivot around to Prince, who's rushing toward us.

The witch in me growls in frustration. I've been waiting for this moment since I stepped foot into this hell. He stops within a few feet of me. He senses I'm ready for a brawl. His tongue curls and his jaws snap as he awaits my reaction. When he realizes I'm not backing down, he charges straight toward me. I take in a breath as he tackles me to the floor. I grab a hold of his neck, gripping as tight as I can. He lands on top and I wrap my legs around his waist. Prince is stuck in between my death grip. I squeeze tighter, wanting to squeeze the life from him. It's not my magic; I'm working off pure anger.

"Ronnie." A voice brings me back as a whimper comes from Prince. Prince falls to the side of me, struggling to breathe. I tighten my grip once more. I want to ensure that he passes out. He holds his hands up, surrendering. Then I let go. Luckily for him, he's still alive. However, any second this mansion will be in flames.

We scurry out the door with James leading the way. We spot Kenny waiting for us. Even with blood running down his face and two black eyes he still looks amazing. I don't bother asking where the guard is. I know the answer. With all my men at my side, I exit the gates of hell. I'm finally free.

EPILOGUE

I sit on the bench staring out in the distance at all three of my guys playing football together. We have become one big, happy family. The grass sways as the sun weaves through the clouds. The snow has melted and spring is quickly approaching.

There is a bigger spot in my heart for Kenny. He is the first guy I saw when I stepped onto campus. It was love at first sight. I'll never let the twins know the truth. I always tell them I love them all the same. Most people don't understand our relationship. It is not traditional, but it works for us.

For now, I feel complete. Headmaster was arrested. Prince never made it out of the house. However, no one ever found his body. Grace and I are even speaking again, now that I live on Mage's campus. We all reside in the same room: Kenny, James, Josh, and myself. They all treat me like the queen I am.

I finally know the truth. Kenny admitted to informing Prince when light faes arrive on campus. He says he needed to do it to survive. And Prince never killed anyone. It was just to feed. I can relate. I guess I did what I needed to feed myself when I lived with my mother. It's all behind us now. We all have a bright future ahead.

****

Quick Author's Note:

For those of you who are new to me. Dragon Burn was my first PNR book. My own labor of love. I was struggling to write PNR because my first book was Urban Fantasy. Not everyone who likes Urban Fantasy likes PNR and vice versa.

So, I struggled with the decision to dip my toe in the PNR world. But, Im glad I did because while Urban Fantasy is my first love I love PNR just as much. I have even written books that are a blend of the both. Urban Fantasy Romance if you will.

A little bit about me. I didn't grow up reading

romance novels. I did read a lot of Judy Blume books in my pre-teens years. Which inspired me to write my first book at the tender age of ten, friend in disguise. The book wasn't good but it did give me the writing bug. Over my teenage years and throughout my life I have always kept a journal. I never had the courage to attempt to write a book let alone several books.

So after months and months of should I write a book or not. In October of 2019, I finally sat my butt in the chair and wrote my first book Eternal Curse. A blend of my love for ghost busters and Buffy the vampire slayer. I love all things paranormal

If you are a paranormal junkie like I am then sign up for my weekly newsletter. I promise not to email you more than once a week.

Included in this weekly newsletter is plenty of wonderful things like, pictures of Connor the cat (My writing buddy), Chances to win awesome prizes, sales and free books, and be the first to here about new releases.

Join me here https://dl.bookfunnel.com/r50466sipa and receive a free novella that you cannot buy on any storefront as my thank you gift for choosing to signup to my newsletter.

. . .

With Love,

R.L. Wilson

P.S. I hope you have not had enough urban fantasy romance yet. Celena has her own pack, Pre-order her book about her escape from Prince and her lamp.

Start Celena's Story

https://books2read.com/u/mZEBeR

ALSO BY R.L. WILSON

Urban Fantasy

The Urban Fae Series

Eternal Love

Eternal Curse

Eternal Fire

Eternal Shadows

Eternal Darkness

Paranormal Romance Series

The Omen Club

Dragon Burn

Dragon Love

Dragon Curse

Dragon Flame

Dragon Blood Coming Soon

Dragon Kiss. Coming Soon

Witch Academy of Ash

Phantom light

Shadow light

Monster light

The Magical Jinn Series: Coming Soon

Celena's Pack Book 1

Celena's Pack Book 2

Celena's Pack Book3

Celenas's Pack Book 4

Celena's Pack Book 5

Coming Soon

Misfit Academy

Supernatural Academy

Nala's Broken Pack Series

STALK ME

Follow me on social media

FB: facebook.com/rlwilson723

Twitter: twitter.com/exquisitenovel1

Instagram: instagram.com/rlwilson23

Tik Tok: https://vm.tiktok.com/ZMJnQnPgY/"

Join my reader group https://www.facebook.com/ groups/440691789814122/

Sign-up for my newsletter https://www. subscribepage.com/f2v6g5

Check out my website
www.rlwilsonauthor.com